OUTLANDS

THE GREAT FOREST

THE ARENA

BARRICADED CITY

THE GREAT FOREST

For J.L. and H.B. who know a lot about dough,
R.L. and K.B. who prefer knights to days,
B.L. and T.B. who love dragons,
and K.K. and A.Z. who breathed fire into this story.
—D. L.

This one's for the parents: Maria and Tony,
to say I'm appreciative would be the world's
greatest understatement.
—G. E.

STERLING CHILDREN'S BOOKS
New York

An Imprint of Sterling Publishing Co., Inc.
1166 Avenue of the Americas
New York, NY 10036

ISBN 978-1-4549-2141-7

Distributed in Canada by Sterling Publishing Co., Inc.
C/o Canadian Manda Group, 664 Annette Street
Toronto, Ontario, Canada M6S 2C8
Distributed in the United Kingdom by GMC Distribution Services
Castle Place, 166 High Street, Lewes, East Sussex, England BN7 1XU
Distributed in Australia by NewSouth Books
45 Beach Street, Coogee, NSW 2034, Australia

For information about custom editions, special sales, and premium and corporate purchases, please contact Sterling Special Sales at
800-805-5489 or specialsales@sterlingpublishing.com.

Manufactured in China
Lot #:
2 4 6 8 10 9 7 5 3 1
07/17

www.sterlingpublishing.com

The artwork for this book was created digitally.

Designed by Irene Vandervoort

Dough Knights AND Dragons

by DEE LEONE

illustrated by
GEORGE ERMOS

STERLING CHILDREN'S BOOKS
New York

IN A MAGICAL KINGDOM far to the east,
lived a very small knight and a very large beast.

One day while collecting fresh herbs in a glen,
the young knight discovered a well-hidden den.

It was filled with ingredients he'd not seen before. The lad couldn't resist—he just had to explore!

In the blink of an eye, he filled a large vat
with a little of this and a little of that.

The pleasing aroma of hot savory stew
woke a shape in the dark that soon came into view.

The knight jumped in fright and feared he'd be caught,
but the beast stopped to drink from the simmering pot.

"This soup is delicious. Can't you stay . . . please?
We'll cook and we'll dine and we'll share recipes."

There was something sincere in the dragon's appeal,
so the knight ceased to think he'd become a hot meal.

The unlikely pair learned they both liked to bake.
They made sea-serpent cookies and unicorn cake!

They created tall castles with sugar and spice,
and stirred up huge helpings of pixie-dust rice.

But in that great kingdom so far to the east,
friendship was outlawed between knight and beast.

When a knight came of age he was bound by a rule
to spear a winged beast in a challenging duel.

And a dragon was also required to fight,
commanded by edict to swallow a knight.

The upcoming match filled the friends with great fear,
for both were required to take part that year.

"I won't spear a dragon," the knight said. "I can't!"
"I won't eat a knight," said the dragon. "I shan't!"

They cooked and they baked and they made a big mess.
Five plates of dessert didn't lessen their stress.

On the eve of the contest they had lots to do.
They were bound and determined to bake something new.

So they mixed and they measured, they kneaded and rolled,
then cut shapes from dough with a circular mold.

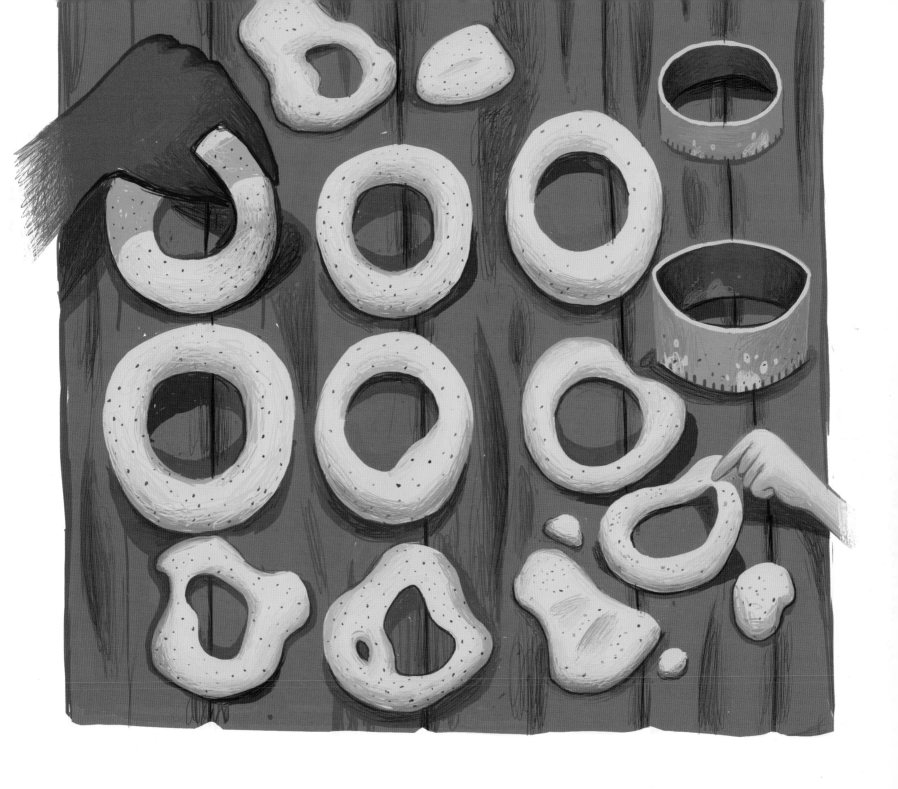

They knew this creation could well be their last
and anxiously worked just a little too fast.

They deep-fried the dough in a kettle of oil.
The dragon's hot breath brought it all to a boil.

The knight speared a shape that resembled a beast,
then he took a small bite and . . . oh, what a feast!

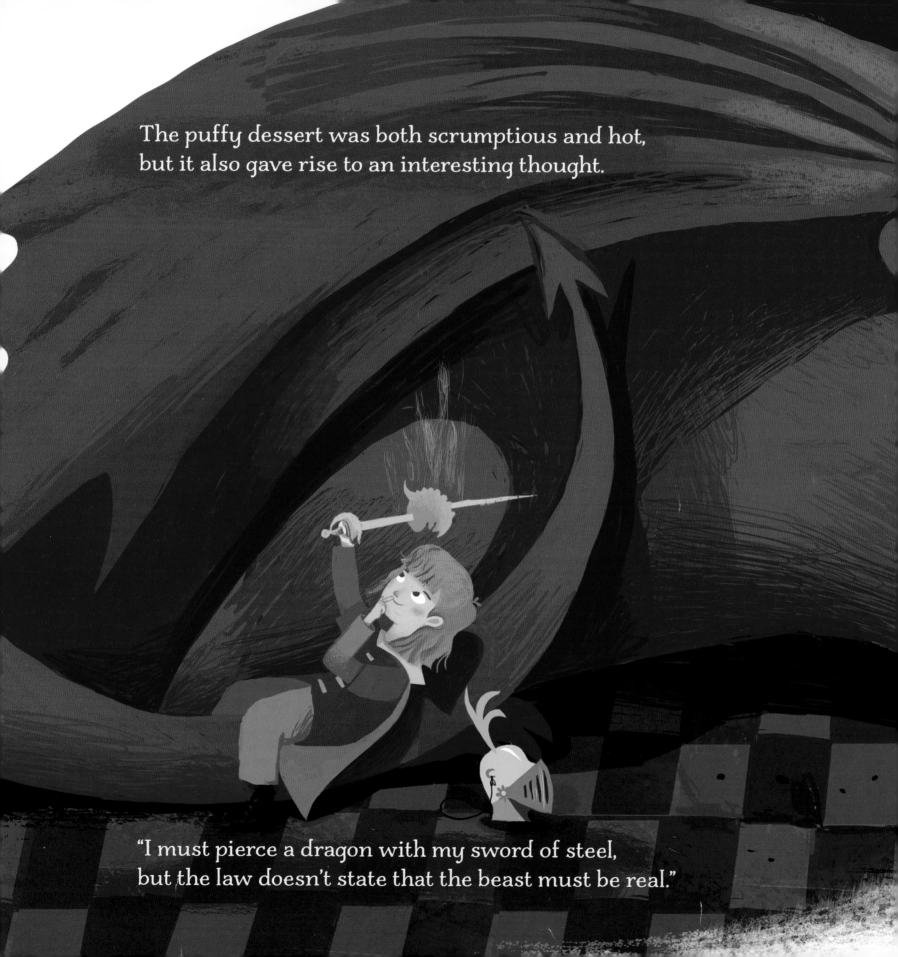

The puffy dessert was both scrumptious and hot,
but it also gave rise to an interesting thought.

"I must pierce a dragon with my sword of steel,
but the law doesn't state that the beast must be real."

"And I am required to swallow a knight.
If he's made of dough, shouldn't that be all right?"

So they melted some armor, quite shiny and bright,
for a cast of a dragon and one of a knight.

They mixed sugar and flour, shortening and yeast.
From the dough, they created each knight and each beast.

Exhausted, they pushed the scraps into a heap,
washed their hands, brushed their teeth,
and fell quickly asleep.

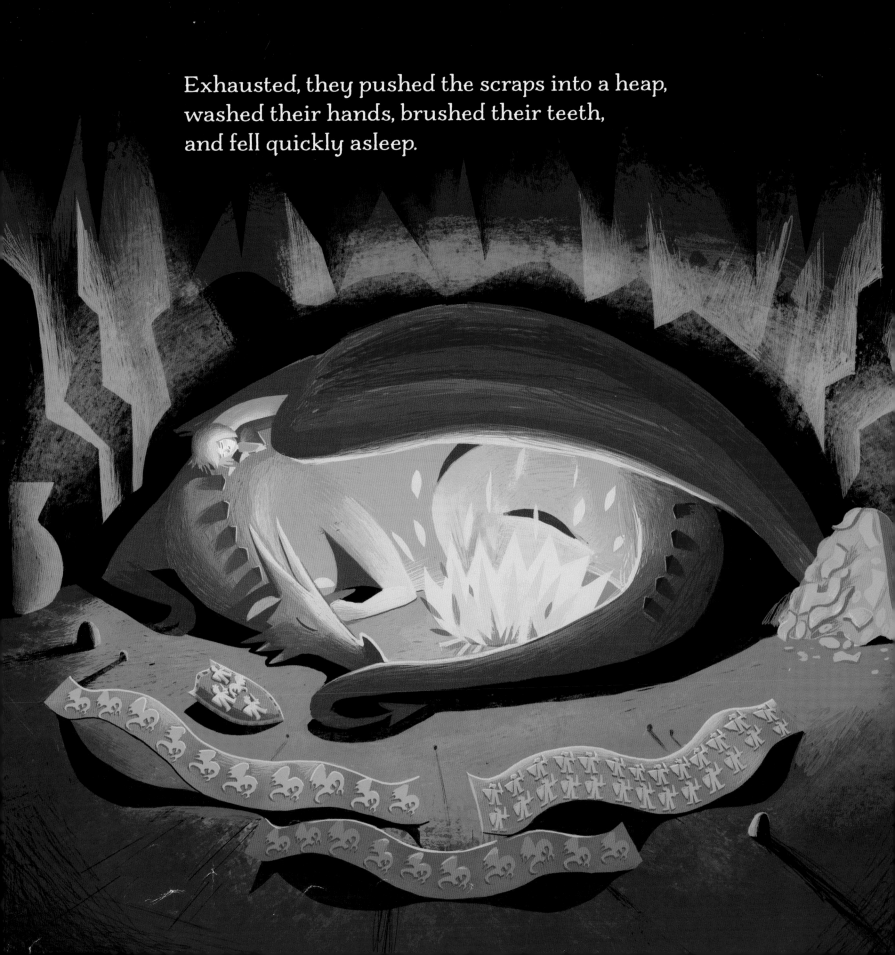

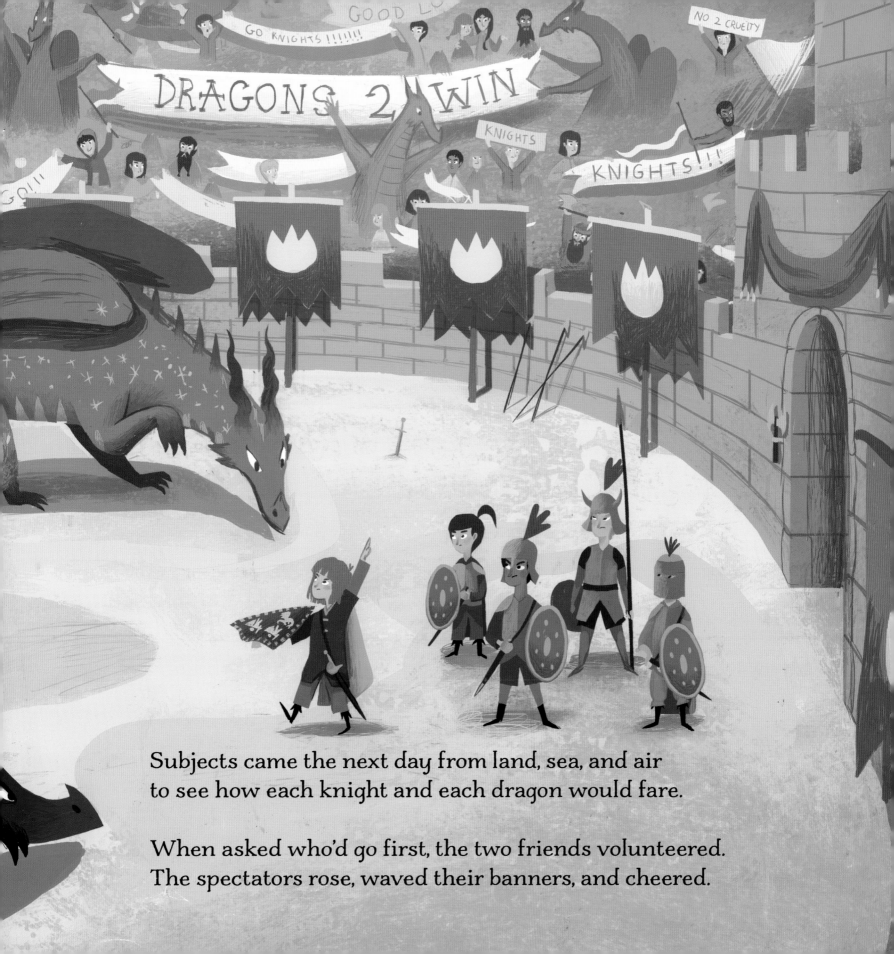

Subjects came the next day from land, sea, and air
to see how each knight and each dragon would fare.

When asked who'd go first, the two friends volunteered.
The spectators rose, waved their banners, and cheered.

The worried contestants stepped onto the field.
Then the knight dropped his sword and laid down his shield.

"He'll be burnt to a crisp!" all the people exclaimed.
"We'll win this first round," every dragon proclaimed.

But the beast didn't aim at the small helpless knight. Instead, he set all of the cooking alight.

The dragon king fumed and the royal king thundered. "What's going on?" the shocked spectators wondered.

When the dough knights were done, the beast swallowed a few, then proceeded to cook all the other shapes, too.

The knight pierced his sword through a dragon with wings, then he and the beast humbly bowed to the kings.

"I speared a winged beast as the law states, my sire."
"And I ate a knight cooked with dragon-breath fire."

"We don't understand why we always must fight."
"We made these together. Please take a bite."

So the dough knights and dragons were given a taste.
The kings ate them all—not a one went to waste!

Because of the heroes, all dueling was banned,
and all kinds of friendships soon spread through the land.

Henceforth, competitions between dragons and knights
consisted of bake-offs and festive food fights.

The
End

FRIENDSHIP HILLS
HOME TO ALL

MAGICAL KINGDOM

OUTLANDS

THE DWARF MOUNTAINS

PIXIE RING

THE NARROW PASS

SERPENT'S TRAIL

GOBLIN'S ISLE